# Tugg
### and
# Teeny

## Jungle Surprises

Written by **J. Patrick Lewis**

Illustrated by **Christopher Denise**

For Sanay, with love,
—Grandpat

This book has a reading comprehension level of 2.8 under the ATOS®
readability formula. For information about ATOS please visit www.renlearn.com.
ATOS is a registered trademark of Renaissance Learning, Inc.

Lexile®, Lexile® Framework and the Lexile® logo are trademarks of MetaMetrics, Inc.,
and are registered in the United States and abroad. The trademarks and names of other
companies and products mentioned herein are the property of their respective owners.
Copyright © 2010 MetaMetrics, Inc. All rights reserved.

## Sleeping Bear Press™

315 E. Eisenhower Parkway, Suite 200
Ann Arbor, MI 48108
www.sleepingbearpress.com

Sleeping Bear Press is an imprint of Gale, a part of Cengage Learning.

Printed and bound in the United States.

10 9 8 7 6 5 4 3 2 1

Printed by Bang Printing, Brainerd, MN, 1ˢᵗ Ptg., 05/2011

Library of Congress Cataloging-in-Publication Data

Lewis, J. Patrick.
Tugg and Teeny : jungle surprises / written by J. Patrick Lewis ;
illustrated by Christopher Denise.
p. cm.
Summary: Tugg, a gorilla, and his best friend Teeny, a monkey,
lead their other friends in three jungle adventures.
ISBN 978-1-58536-515-9 (case)  ISBN 978-1-58536-686-6 (pbk)
[1. Gorilla—Fiction. 2. Monkeys—Fiction. 3. Jungle animals—Fiction. 4. Best friends—Fiction. 5.
Friendship—Fiction.] I. Denise, Christopher, ill. II. Title.
PZ7.L5866Tuj 2011
[E]—dc22    2010041823

# Table of Contents

# A Great Gusting Mystery

"What a perfect day to stay inside and work on my next poem," said Teeny. "Now if I could just find my lucky writing hat."

"Where did you see it last?" asked Tugg.

"Yesterday it was on the porch but it is not there now," Teeny said.

"Let's play detectives, Teeny," said Tugg. "I'm sure we will be able to find it."

When they came to the waterhole,

Pinkie Flamingo looked very sad.

"I am sorry but I have not seen your

lucky hat, Teeny," she said, "and my prettiest

feather has disappeared."

"Follow us then," said Tugg, "on the

great hat and feather hunt."

"Have you seen Teeny's hat?" Tugg asked Flap the Elephant.

"No," said Flap. "Have you seen my umbrella? Elephants are supposed to have good memories, but I forgot where I put it."

"Okay, Flap," said Tugg. "We will help you find your umbrella."

"Will you help me too, Tugg?" asked

Margie Barge. "I set my inner tube on the

shore of the waterhole, and the next thing

I knew, it was gone!"

"Join us, the Jungle Detectives, Margie," said Tugg. "We are happy to help another friend and together we will find our treasures."

So they walked up and down the jungle.

And they asked everyone they met.

But no one had seen a thing.

Everyone started to bicker and argue about who had taken the missing items.

Just as they were ready to give up and go home, a big gust of wind blew up.

To escape the blustery wind, they all huddled under a tall tree.

Tugg shouted, "Look up there! You have solved the mystery at last, you brilliant detectives!"

He said, "Now we know who took Teeny's hat and Pinkie's feather and Flap's umbrella and Margie's inner tube.

"It was that sneaky fellow, the wind."

# The Zig-Zag Race

Teeny and Tugg had just finished dinner when they heard hoofbeats outside their window.

Zig and Zag, the wacky zebra brothers, were running to the waterhole.

Teeny shouted, "Hey, which one of you
is faster?"

The brothers stopped and looked at
each other. "Who knows?" they said.

"Why don't we have a race to find out?"
said Teeny.

"I hope Zag wins," said Teeny. "What about you, Tuggboat?"

"They are both fast runners, Monkeyface," said Tugg. "May the best zebra win."

Rory Lion gave the starter roar, and the

zebras were off!

First one, then the other took the lead.

Zig, Zag,

Zig, Zag.

Back and forth, neck and neck.

Teeny got dizzy just watching them.

The whole jungle cheered wildly.

It was a very close race, but at the finish

line, one zebra pulled ahead of the other.

Teeny cried, "Who won?"

"I am not sure who won," said Tugg.

They ran over to where the zebra

brothers stood, out of breath.

Tugg yelled, "Wait! Who won?"

"I did!" answered both brothers.

"But you two look exactly the same.

Who is who?"

"That's easy," said one brother. "I have black stripes on white."

"And I have white stripes on black," said the other.

"But you both have the *same* black and white stripes," said Teeny.

"You also look exactly alike *from behind*," said Tugg.

Just then Dr. Giraffe walked up.

"Only a zebra can tell one zebra from another," he said. "But try this simple trick to tell Zig from Zag: Whenever you meet them, just tell a funny story."

"A funny story?" asked Teeny.

Turning to Zig and Zag, Teeny began, "Once upon a time there were two wacky zebra brothers ..."

Right away the zebras started laughing out loud.

"There, you see?" said Dr. Giraffe. "Zag has something that Zig does not have."

"But wait," said Teeny. "We still don't know who won the race."

"Who cares!" Zig and Zag shouted together.

And from that time on everyone knew how to tell Zig and Zag apart.

# Wind-Fishing

"Tugg, what kind of bird has polka-dot wings and a wiggly tail?" asked Teeny.

Tugg looked up in the sky. He knew that it was not really a bird, but he wanted to tease Teeny.

"That's a Belong Bird," said Tugg. "In a minute it will *be long gone*! Just a little gorilla joke, Monkeyface. Let's go see if we can find it."

In a clearing they found some of their

neighbors. Everyone was looking up at the

strange bird in the sky.

Milly Heron asked, "Is it green and blue with a crooked tail?"

"No, it is red and yellow with a straight tail," said Rory Lion.

BooBoo the Baboon said, "Then it must be a parrot."

"It is too high to be a parrot," said Go-Go Gazelle.

"Then it is an airplane," said Zig, the wacky zebra brother.

"It is too small to be an airplane," said Zag, the other wacky zebra brother.

Everyone was quiet for a long time. No one knew for sure what was up in the sky.

"Where is Violet?" asked Tugg. "She will know what it is."

So everyone marched over to Violet's
house. But the warthog was not at home.
Instead they found Chuckie Cheetah.

"Chuckie," asked Tugg, "where is Violet?"

"Wind-fishing."

"*Wind-fishing?*" Teeny scratched her head. "What is that?"

"I have no idea," said Chuckie. "Violet just said she was hoping to catch a strong wind."

At last, there was Violet lying in a heap

of jungle grass, whistling and holding onto

a piece of string that went straight up to

the sky.

"Look!" yelled Teeny. "Violet really *is* wind-fishing. Her fishing line goes all the way up to the sky."

"What are you fishing for, Violet?" Tugg asked her. "And have you seen a strange bird?"

Violet tugged on the string until

something fluttered down and landed right

in front of Teeny.

Everyone gasped, "Violet, you caught the bird!"

Violet burped. "It's a *kite* bird," she said. "Now, who wants to fly it?"

And everyone spent the rest of the

afternoon wind-fishing with Violet's kite.